Maybelle
and the
Haunted Cupcake

Read all about Maybelle's
other adventures!

Maybelle Goes to Tea

Maybelle in the Soup

Maybelle Goes to School

Maybelle

and the
Haunted Cupcake

Katie Speck

illustrations by

Paul Rátz de Tagyos

SQUARE
FISH

Henry Holt and Company ⑨ New York

For my grandmother
—K. S.

SQUARE
FISH

An imprint of Macmillan Publishing Group, LLC
175 Fifth Avenue
New York, NY 10010
mackids.com

Square Fish and the Square Fish logo are trademarks of Macmillan and
are used by Henry Holt and Company, LLC under license from Macmillan.

Square Fish books may be purchased for business or promotional use.
For information on bulk purchases, please contact the Macmillan Corporate
and Premium Sales Department at (800) 221-7945 x5442 or by
e-mail at specialmarkets@macmillan.com.

Library of Congress Cataloging-in-Publication Data Available
ISBN 978-1-250-06277-2 (paperback) / ISBN 978-1-4299-6399-2 (ebook)

Originally published in the United States by Henry Holt and Company, LLC
This Square Fish Edition: 2015
Square Fish logo designed by Filomena Tuosto

10 9 8 7 6 5 4

AR: 3.3 / LEXILE: 510L

Contents

⊙ 1 ⊙

Make a Wish

At last it was evening at Number 10 Grand Street. In the afternoon, Myrtle Peabody had baked Mystery Ingredient Miniature Cupcakes for the Ladies' Annual Bake Sale. She had decorated them JUST SO with pink icing and chopped nuts and chocolate sprinkles. Now she arranged them on a platter for her husband, Herbert, to admire.

Watching from her cozy little home under the refrigerator, Maybelle the Cockroach waved her antennae. "Yum! I know what I want for dinner. I'm going to have a taste of those cupcakes," she said to her friend Henry the Flea.

"Just remember The Rules, Maybelle."

Maybelle recited them by heart: *"When it's light, stay out of sight; if you're spied, better hide; never meet with human feet.* Don't worry. I'll wait until it's safe,

Henry. But why does getting something to eat have to be so hard?"

"It isn't," Henry said. "It's easy. I live on Ramona, and when I get hungry, I bite her." Ramona was the Peabodys' cat. She was napping close by on the kitchen floor.

"That's fine for you," Maybelle said. "But I'm tired of going out for food and

worrying about The Rules and being chased by Ramona. I wish I could eat at home. I wish someone would bring food to me right here."

"Be careful what you wish for, Maybelle. Sometimes wishes come true," Henry said.

Maybelle would soon find out what he meant.

☙ 2 ❧

Crown Her!

"**A**CHOO!"

The friends looked at each other.

"Did you sneeze?" Maybelle said to Henry.

"No. Did you?"

"A-A-ACHOO! I did, sweetie. I'm Bernice."

Bernice was a picnic ant with a very bad head cold.

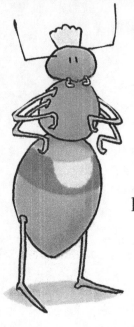

"Sorry to be a bother." Bernice sniffed loudly. "My head is so stuffed up I can't smell my way back to my nest. Mind if I work around here for a while?"

"What sort of work do you do?" Maybelle asked.

"I'll be going out for food and carrying it back here, like I do at home. You just put up your feet and relax. ACHOO!" Bernice started out into the kitchen.

"Wait!" Maybelle said. "There are Rules." She explained them one by one. "We can't go out until the Peabodys have turned off the lights and gone up to bed.

If they see us, they'll call the Bug Man."

"Look, sugar," Bernice said, "I bring food to the nest for the Queen. That's what I do. So, what can I get for you?"

"For *me*? I'm not the Queen!" said Maybelle.

"You'll have to do," Bernice said, and off she went.

Now that Maybelle thought about it, she could picture herself looking ever so fetching in a crown and robe. "I'm the Queen, Henry. And someone is going to wait on me. I've just been wishing for that very thing!"

But of course the Peabodys insisted that there be absolutely, positively NO BUGS at Number 10 Grand Street. And a picnic ant marching around and gathering food for Maybelle under the Peabodys' noses was sure to cause an Extermination Event sooner or later.

"Uh-oh," Henry said.

☙ 3 ☙

A Secret Is a Secret

Maybelle and Henry watched Bernice set off across the kitchen floor right past Ramona's whiskers. Luckily, the cat was still napping and didn't see her. Neither

did the Peabodys. They were admiring Mrs. Peabody's cupcakes. She had tried out a brand-new recipe of her very own, with a Mystery Ingredient.

"Your cupcakes are Perfection, dear," Mr. Peabody said to his wife. "I am sure they will be the hit of the Ladies' Annual Bake Sale tomorrow."

"And, Herbert, no one knows the Mystery Ingredient but me. No one ever will. A secret is a secret."

While the Peabodys talked, Bernice searched for bits of food around their feet. Maybelle and Henry held their breath and watched. Those feet were very large and very useful for squashing bugs. But Bernice didn't seem to notice. She was busy finding food for the Queen. She picked up a lovely chocolate sprinkle.

"She's bringing me a sprinkle, Henry!" Maybelle said. "Chocolate is my favorite!"

"She'd better hurry. Look." Henry pointed to Ramona. She was beginning to wake up from her nap. Her eyes were still closed. But she yawned and stretched out her claws.

"Come back, Bernice! Fast!" the bugs called.

Bernice couldn't smell her way back to her own home. And she couldn't smell her way to Maybelle's, either. "ACHOO!" Carrying the sprinkle, she began wandering around the kitchen, lost and sneezing.

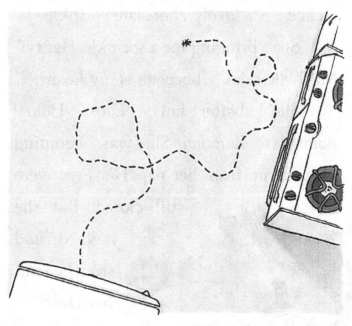

⊙ 4 ⊙

A Close Call

"This way!" the bugs shouted. Maybelle and Henry jumped up and down and waved their legs to get the ant's attention.

In all the commotion, Ramona opened her eyes. "Hiss!" she said. *A tasty little picnic ant!* She began creeping after Bernice, getting nearer and nearer.

Her whiskers trembled with excitement. Her tail twitched.

"Look, dear. Ramona is stalking something." Mrs. Peabody leaned over and squinted. "Ick! It's a *bug*, Herbert! There are absolutely, positively NO BUGS at Number 10 Grand Street. I won't have it!" She snatched Ramona off the floor. "You mustn't touch that nasty thing, Precious."

"Raow," Ramona said.

Mr. Peabody put on his reading

glasses and examined Bernice himself. "It is just one ant, dearest. But where there is one ant, there will be many. I'll go get Something to Take Care of the Problem."

"Please do, dear," Mrs. Peabody said. "I will not remain in the same room with a bug." Mrs. Peabody took herself and her cat upstairs. Ramona's tail was still twitching.

With the Peabodys and their cat gone, Maybelle and Henry rushed out into the kitchen and led Bernice back to the refrigerator.

"That was close!" Maybelle said. "The chocolate sprinkle is very nice, Bernice. But it's much too dangerous for you out there until it gets dark."

"Nonsense. ACHOO! Put your legs up and relax, honey. I saw a little glob of icing that would be real nice with that sprinkle."

Before Maybelle and Henry could stop her, Bernice was gone again.

๑ 5 ๑

A Sticky Situation

Number 10 Grand Street was settled for the night. Henry was dining on Ramona. The Peabodys were in bed. And a plate of cupcakes sat on the kitchen counter in the comforting dark.

It was Maybelle's favorite time of day. But she wasn't happy. She was hungry. She'd been saving her sprinkle to eat with the icing Bernice had promised her. Now she felt grumpy about the slow service. She was the Queen, after all. So she went out to find the ant who was supposed to be waiting on her.

Before she had gone far, she saw Mr. Peabody's solution to the ant problem. It was a charming little trap. ANT COTTAGE—COME IN AND STICK AROUND, the sign on it said. A familiar voice came from inside.

"ACHOO! Get me out of here!"

Maybelle peeked in and saw Bernice stuck to the floor. She couldn't move a leg.

"Sweetie, I've been on some sticky floors, but this one takes the prize," Bernice said.

"Oh dear." Maybelle was supposed to be relaxing with her legs up. "I suppose

I'll have to unstick you." After all, what is a queen without someone waiting on her? Besides, bugs help bugs.

But Maybelle knew if she tried to walk across the floor of the trap to help Bernice, she would get stuck, too. In the morning, Mr. Peabody would find them both. So she crawled up the wall to the ceiling.

"I'm going to hang from the ceiling

and grab you, Bernice. Then I'll pull you up on the word *chocolate*. Ready? Raspberries, whipped cream, CHOCOLATE!"

Maybelle pulled as hard as she could. *SNAP!* Bernice's legs popped free of the floor.

At that very moment, Henry shouted—

"CAT ALERT!"

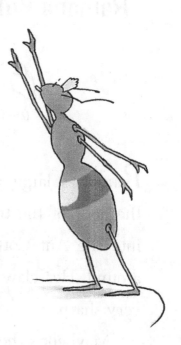

◎ 6 ◎

Ramona Puts Her Foot in It

Ramona's large green eye appeared at the door of the trap. She reached a paw into the Ant Cottage and began to feel around. Her claws were out. They were very sharp.

Maybelle's heart was pounding so hard she thought Ramona might hear it. Ramona felt one wall, then the other. Just when Maybelle was sure that the paw would find her and Bernice on the ceiling, Ramona felt the floor.

"Raow," she said. She tried to pull her paw out. It was stuck.

"Raow!" she said. She gave the trap a shake. Her paw was still stuck.

"RAOW!!!" she said, and began banging wildly around the kitchen, trying to get the Ant Cottage off.

 The Peabodys had just fallen asleep when the racket awakened Mrs. Peabody.

"Herbert, get up! There's someone downstairs," she said, poking her husband.

"Nonsense, dear. Go back to sleep."

Mr. Peabody pulled the covers over his head.

Mrs. Peabody turned on her bedside lamp. "Herbert, I insist. I heard alarming noises. You must investigate!"

Mr. Peabody yawned, put on his robe, and started downstairs.

Meanwhile, with a "RAOW! RAOW!" Ramona shook off the trap and sent it skidding across the floor. It came to rest with Maybelle and Bernice still clinging to its ceiling.

@ 7 @

Peek-a-Boo!

By the time Mr. Peabody reached the kitchen, the house was quiet again. Ramona was licking her paw.

On the ceiling of the Ant Cottage, Bernice was restless. "I can't be hanging around like this, sweetie. I have a job to do."

"Shhhhhh!" Maybelle hissed softly. "There's a human out there. Don't move."

Mr. Peabody looked around. The kitchen was as Mrs. Peabody had left it— JUST SO. "As I suspected," he said to no one in particular. "It was dear Myrtle's imagination. I'm going back to bed."

Before he did, he picked up the trap and peered in to see if he'd caught an ant or two. Maybelle was as still as she could be. She didn't even breathe. And she hoped Bernice beside her wouldn't pick this moment to go back to work.

Mr. Peabody's huge eyeball rolled this way and that. There were no bugs stuck to the floor. No bugs on one wall or the other. He was just about to look at the ceiling when Mrs. Peabody called from upstairs.

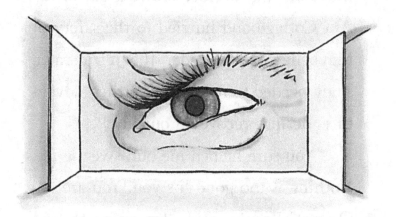

"Herbert dear, is everything all right down there?"

"Yes, Myrtle, everything is JUST SO. Go back to sleep." Mr. Peabody put the trap back on the floor. "This trap didn't catch a thing," he muttered. "I intend to demand my money back."

When he had gone upstairs again, Maybelle and Bernice crawled out of the Ant Cottage and hurried to the safety of Maybelle's home under the refrigerator. They needed to recover from their adventure. Bernice recovered quickly.

"You sure helped me out, sweetie-pie. Nothing is too good for you. You are the Queen!" Bernice said. "I'm going to find you something Real Special. You just put your feet up and relax."

"Don't you ever take a little break?" Maybelle said. She was getting worn out with relaxing.

"Don't be silly, honey. It's no trouble at all. ACHOO!"

Bernice trooped out into the kitchen again.

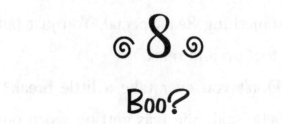

Boo?

What will she bring me this time? Maybelle wondered. *Maybe a nut or two, or the icing she promised, to eat with the sprinkle.* Because Maybelle knew better than to let Bernice out of her sight, she stood at her door and watched the ant cross the kitchen floor.

In the dark kitchen, Ramona watched, too. Her whiskers trembled. Her tail twitched. When she saw Bernice march up a cabinet door, she crouched, ready to attack.

"Not again!" Maybelle said. She was supposed to be enjoying the life of a queen. But she had to take the cat's mind off snacking on Bernice. She skittered out from the safety of her doorway, rushed up behind Ramona, and . . . stopped. What could she do?

"Tickle her tail. She'll hate it," Henry said from somewhere in Ramona's fur.

So Maybelle did the only thing a cockroach can do to a cat. She tickled her. She tickled Ramona's tail

with all six of her legs. Then she ran back home as fast as those legs would carry her.

Ramona was just about to pounce when she felt Maybelle's legs. She was so annoyed that she leaped up and missed Bernice entirely. Instead, her sharp claws sank into the dish towel hanging JUST SO on the cabinet knob. It fell on her head and covered her from head to paw.

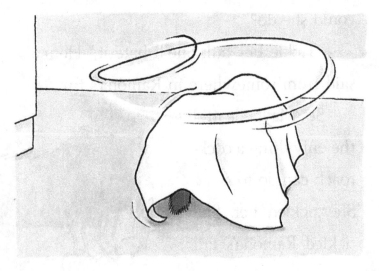

"Meow?" Ramona said. "MEOW!" She couldn't see a thing. So she dashed around the kitchen in a panic.

Upstairs, Mr. Peabody had just gotten back to sleep when Mrs. Peabody poked him again.

"Herbert, wake up! There are strange noises coming from downstairs."

"It's nothing, Myrtle, just like before. Go back to sleep."

Mrs. Peabody turned on the bedside lamp. "I will not close my eyes until you go check," she said firmly.

At that very moment, Ramona howled and tore into the bedroom and out again, still under the dish towel.

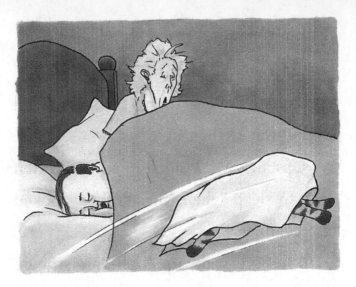

Mrs. Peabody dove under the covers. "It's a ghost!" she shrieked.

Mr. Peabody caught a glimpse of the dish towel disappearing down the hall. "There are no such things as ghosts," he said. "Besides, even if there were, that one is too short to worry about. I'm going back to sleep." And he did.

Mrs. Peabody lay in the dark with her eyes open.

9

Bernice Aims High

"How is a fellow supposed to sleep around here?" Henry said, standing at Maybelle's door.

The dish towel had fallen off Ramona as she fled back down the stairs. Now she was on the windowsill giving herself a long bath to restore her dignity. Henry was wet and grumpy.

"Where is Bernice?" he asked.

Maybelle had last seen Bernice heading up the cabinet door. "She says she's getting me Something Special, Henry."

"Then I think we'd better keep an eye on her, kiddo," Henry said.

So while Ramona bathed, the two friends crept out into the kitchen to see what Bernice was up to. What they saw stopped them in their tracks.

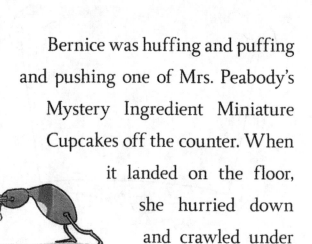

Bernice was huffing and puffing and pushing one of Mrs. Peabody's Mystery Ingredient Miniature Cupcakes off the counter. When it landed on the floor, she hurried down and crawled under it. Then Maybelle and Henry heard her grunt with effort, and the cupcake rose and began to walk.

Maybelle was pleased. "Look what she's getting me, Henry! That cupcake is all for me," she said.

"That cupcake is trouble, kiddo."

And indeed it was. Because Bernice was lost. She didn't know which direction to go. She couldn't smell a thing.

"ACHOO!"

Ramona looked up from her bath to see a cupcake staggering aimlessly around the kitchen. "HISS!" she said. She arched her back. Each hair on her body stuck straight out.

Every cat knows that cupcakes do not walk. So Ramona dashed up the stairs and onto the Peabodys' bed.

☙ 10 ☙

The Haunted Cupcake

Mr. Peabody had just begun to snore when Mrs. Peabody poked him.

"Herbert, wake up! I think Ramona has seen a ghost!"

Mr. Peabody put his pillow over his head.

Mrs. Peabody poked him harder. "I tell you Ramona has seen a ghost, Herbert! Every hair on her body is sticking straight

out. I will not sleep a wink until you go downstairs and check."

Mr. Peabody sighed, got out of bed, and started down the stairs.

"Wait for us, Herbert!" Mrs. Peabody hurried into her fuzzy pink robe and slippers. "You can't leave us alone with a ghost in the house," she said.

So Mrs. Peabody held Ramona and

clutched Mr. Peabody, and they all went downstairs together.

Maybelle and Henry heard the Peabodys coming. The bugs had only seconds to get to safety. Maybelle wanted the cupcake with pink icing and chopped nuts and sprinkles, but she did *not* want a visit from the Bug Man. They needed to get under the refrigerator—fast.

"This way, Bernice! Drop the cupcake and run!" Maybelle cried.

Bernice was busy. "I'll be right along. You just go put your legs up and relax, sugar," she said, heading first one way and then another. "It's no trouble at all."

But Henry had been right. The cupcake *was* trouble.

The Peabodys were at the kitchen door now. There was nothing Maybelle and Henry could do but dash for cover under Mrs. Peabody's cupcake and help Bernice carry it.

"All right, everybody! Lift and run!"

little Henry cried, even though he had trouble reaching the cupcake at all.

At the door, Mr. Peabody flipped on the light. For a moment, the only thing the Peabodys and their cat did was stare. One of Mrs. Peabody's dainty pink cupcakes was struggling across the kitchen floor toward the refrigerator.

"My cupcakes are haunted!" Mrs. Peabody gasped, barely remaining upright.

Ramona's fur stuck out even straighter than before.

Mr. Peabody held up his wife and tried to calm her. "There must be some other explanation, dearest," he said. "Cupcakes do not walk."

"A Haunted Cupcake does!" Mrs. Peabody's voice quivered. "I will not remain in the same room with a ghost. Get me out of here, Herbert!"

Mr. Peabody helped his wife outside and left her on the front lawn. "Wait here, Myrtle. I'll deal with this," he said.

He went to face the cupcake alone.

☙ 11 ❧

On the Run

On the lawn, Mrs. Peabody and Ramona were joined by their next-door neighbor, Sue Ellen Snerdly.

"I couldn't help but notice you standing outside in the middle of the night," Sue Ellen said. "What is the matter, Myrtle?"

"My Mystery Ingredient Miniature Cupcakes are walking," Mrs. Peabody said.

Mrs. Snerdly patted Mrs. Peabody's arm. "Everyone knows that cupcakes do not walk, dear."

"Mine do! My cupcakes are haunted!" Mrs. Peabody said. She was quite definite.

"Surely there is some other explanation. Perhaps you used too much cinnamon." Sue Ellen always tried to be helpful.

"I didn't use any cinnamon at all!"

"Oh my! Then *whatever* did you put in your cupcakes that might cause them to walk, Myrtle?"

That's just what Herbert Peabody was trying to find out.

Mr. Peabody tiptoed ever so lightly after the cupcake, wielding a frying pan for protection. It never hurt to be prepared.

Maybelle, Henry, and Bernice were moving as fast as they could across the kitchen floor. But carrying a cupcake— even a miniature one—was hard work. They were much too slow to escape from Mr. Peabody. Maybelle looked back and saw his great big feet close behind them . . . and getting closer.

"Run! Run!" she said. They had almost reached her home. If they could go just a little faster . . .

Mr. Peabody bent over the cupcake and raised the frying pan high above his head, ready to strike. But at that very moment, the cupcake bumped up against the refrigerator. Maybelle, Henry, and Bernice scrambled out from under it and through Maybelle's door to safety.

☙ 12 ☙

A Secret Is Still a Secret

Mr. Peabody lifted the cupcake. There was nothing under it, nothing at all. He put it back on the floor and nudged it with his toe. It didn't walk. It didn't move an inch. He scratched his head and went back outside.

"Well, dear, your cupcakes *are* haunted after all."

"What did I tell you, Herbert!" said Mrs. Peabody.

"But they seem to have settled down for the night." Mr. Peabody yawned. "It's safe to go back to bed now, dearest."

Sue Ellen Snerdly was aflutter with excitement. "Your Haunted Cupcakes will be the talk of the Ladies' Annual Bake Sale tomorrow, Myrtle!"

Mrs. Peabody hadn't thought of that. It was true. She and her cupcakes would be the center of attention. How lovely! It had been a terrifying night, but she was suddenly feeling quite herself again.

"May I *please* know what the Mystery Ingredient in your cupcakes is, Myrtle?"

"That is my secret, Sue Ellen. And a secret is a secret. But you may come by in the morning before the bake sale and taste a Haunted Cupcake. If you're not afraid, of course."

"Oh, thank you, Myrtle!" Sue Ellen said.

"You're quite welcome, dear. Now Herbert and I really must go back inside," Mrs. Peabody said. "There are bugs out here."

☙ 13 ☙

All Clear

Safe in Maybelle's little home under the refrigerator, the bugs caught their breath. Bernice sniffed. And then she sniffed once more.

"My goodness! I can smell again! I do believe all that running around has cleared my head."

"Does that mean you'll be going home?" Maybelle tried not to sound too relieved.

"Why, yes. I'll be getting on back to my nest now. Can you manage without me?"

"Yes, thank you. I think so. But it will be hard," Maybelle said. She didn't want to hurt Bernice's feelings.

"I'll be going along then. Good-bye!" Bernice was heading out the door when she stopped and turned back. "I notice you haven't eaten your sprinkle, sweetie. Mind if I take it with me?"

"No, you can have it, Bernice," said Maybelle. She sighed. "I'm too tired to eat it anyway."

"Thanks, honey. You make a nice queen. But you really should learn to relax."

Bernice marched off with the sprinkle. And for the first time that evening, Maybelle put her legs up. "Being waited on is a lot of trouble, Henry. I think I'd rather do for myself from now on."

"Good for you, kiddo. You don't have it so bad. You still have those cupcakes to look forward to. As for me, all the excitement has made me hungry. I'm going to find Ramona." Henry headed out the door. "She's all right, but I wish I had a dog."

"Be careful what you wish for, Henry," Maybelle said. Henry didn't hear her. He was already gone.

With the Peabodys and Ramona snoring upstairs and the Haunted Cupcakes waiting for her on the counter, Maybelle settled down for a little nap before dinner.

She dozed off thinking about the sprinkle she'd get. For herself. As soon as she rested up from being the Queen.

Go Fish!

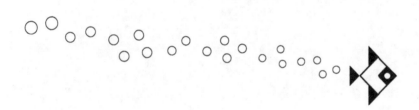

GOFISH

KATIE SPECK

What did you want to be when you grew up?
When I was very little I wanted to grow up to be a horse. I didn't.

When did you realize you wanted to be a writer?
I always wanted to be a writer. It just took me a very long time to get started.

What's your most embarrassing childhood memory?
When I was six or so, I took part in a potato race at a birthday party. The prize was a ukulele. I wanted that thing. So when we were given forks to balance our potatoes on, I stuck my fork in my potato and won the race. Everyone knew what I'd done, but they gave me the prize anyway. I was so ashamed of myself that I haven't touched a ukulele since.

What's your favorite childhood memory?
Impossible question. I had a wonderful childhood.

As a young person, who did you look up to most?
My father. Then and since.

What was your favorite thing about school?
Anything that had to do with words. And lunch. I loved lunch.

What were your hobbies as a kid? What are your hobbies now?
Reading, drawing, climbing trees, and early on, riding my hobby horse. Why walk if you can canter?

Did you play sports as a kid?
Not much. I tended to be the last kid chosen for ball games. So while I sat on the bench, I would imagine galloping a fierce black stallion onto the field of play. I still love that idea!

Where do you write your books?
The Maybelle books begin in the bathtub while I stare at the ceiling. If I get an idea that I think is funny, usually just one line of dialogue, one scene, I begin building a story around it on index cards that I keep next to my bed. The story doesn't make it to my desk until it's just about a done deal.

What sparked your imagination for the Maybelle books?
My grandmother, who imagined a cockroach named Maybelle and entertained two generations of children with her.

If you were a bug, what kind would you want to be?
A cockroach, of course!

What was your favorite book when you were a kid? Do you have a favorite book now?
When I was ten or eleven, I read a book called *The Chestry Oak* by Kate Seredy. I read it in one sitting, finished it in the middle of the night, and cried so hard when I was done that I woke up my parents.

One of my favorite books now is *The Miraculous Journey of Edward Tulane* by Kate DiCamillo. I must like to cry.

What's the best advice you have ever received about writing?
Do it!

Do you ever get writer's block? What do you do to get back on track?
I specialize in writer's block. Hot baths, music, and a stern talking-to—by me to myself—usually help. And the support of other writers.

What do you want readers to remember about your books?
That my books made them laugh.

What do you consider to be your greatest accomplishment?
That I wrote stories about a cockroach worthy of pearls and a bow—and publication!

What would your readers be most surprised to learn about you?
I'm as squeamish about cockroaches as anyone else. EEEEK!

Maybelle is back!
And now for a schooltime
adventure in search of none
other than . . . cake!

Maybelle
Goes to
School

Katie Speck

Illustrated by
Paul Rátz de Tagyos

Keep reading for a sneak peek.

❂ 1 ❂

The Tower of Taste

Maybelle the Cockroach was obeying all The Rules: *When it's light, stay out of sight; if you're spied, better hide; never meet with human feet.* She hadn't had an adventure in some time. That suited her fine. She wasn't fond of adventures.

She was fond of cake.

One evening, Maybelle watched from her home under the refrigerator while

Myrtle Peabody baked and frosted her famous Ten-Layer Tower of Taste. Mrs. Peabody was quite sure there were ABSOLUTELY, POSITIVELY NO BUGS at Number 10 Grand Street. She left the cake uncovered on the kitchen counter.

Maybelle thought Mrs. Peabody's cake was the most beautiful thing she had ever seen. She intended to have a bite. Or two.

"Don't worry," she said to her friend Henry the Flea. Henry lived and dined on Ramona, the Peabodys' cat. "It's dark.

No one will see me and call the Bug Man. And I won't be squashed, either; the Peabodys' feet will be in bed."

"Keep your eyes open, kiddo," Henry said. "It's easy to fall asleep when you eat too much. You could wake up on that cake and find yourself in Trouble." Henry would know. He once went to sleep on a poodle after a tasty meal. He almost got a flea dip.

"I won't fall asleep," Maybelle said. "There's a different fruit jam between every layer of that cake. I'm going to sample them all and be home before morning."

Henry looked at the Tower of Taste. "What's the special occasion, I wonder?"

Maybelle should have wondered, too. When a cake rises to ten layers, Something is up.

☽ 2 ☾

The Light Dawns

Z Z Z Z

After everyone was asleep, Maybelle
scuttled out into the dark kitchen and up
onto the counter.

Mrs. Peabody's cake rose high
in the air. Maybelle began at the
bottom and tasted her way up.
She sampled pink icing and
sugar flowers.

And she did exactly

what Henry had warned her not to do: she ate too much and fell asleep. By morning she snored softly in the blueberry jam between the fourth and fifth layers of the Tower of Taste.

Meanwhile, as the sun came up, the Peabodys began bustling around the house.

While Henry hid on Ramona's belly, Mr. Peabody brushed the cat's black stripes. "Ramona must surely be the prettiest, shiniest tabby cat anywhere," he said. He tied a red bow around her neck JUST SO to make it official. She did not look pleased.

Mrs. Peabody set

her cake on a platter and arranged candied fruit on top in a little pile, JUST SO.

"My cake will be the grandest one at the elementary school bake sale this year," she said to Mr. Peabody. Mrs. Peabody never passed up a chance to show off. "The Tower of Taste will put Mildred Snodgrass's cake to shame."

"ABSOLUTELY, POSITIVELY!" the Peabodys said together.

Right then, Maybelle woke up where she had no business being and knew she was in Trouble.